T is for Texas
Copyright © 2015 by Dry Climate Inc.

Printed in China

First edition-2nd printing

www.dryclimatestudios.com

ISBN
978-0-9906858-7-6

Library of Congress Control Number
2015930057

T is for Texas

Written by Maria Kernahan
Illustrated by Michael Schafbuch

A is for armadillo, with a long pointy nose.

A baby has a softer shell that gets harder as it grows.

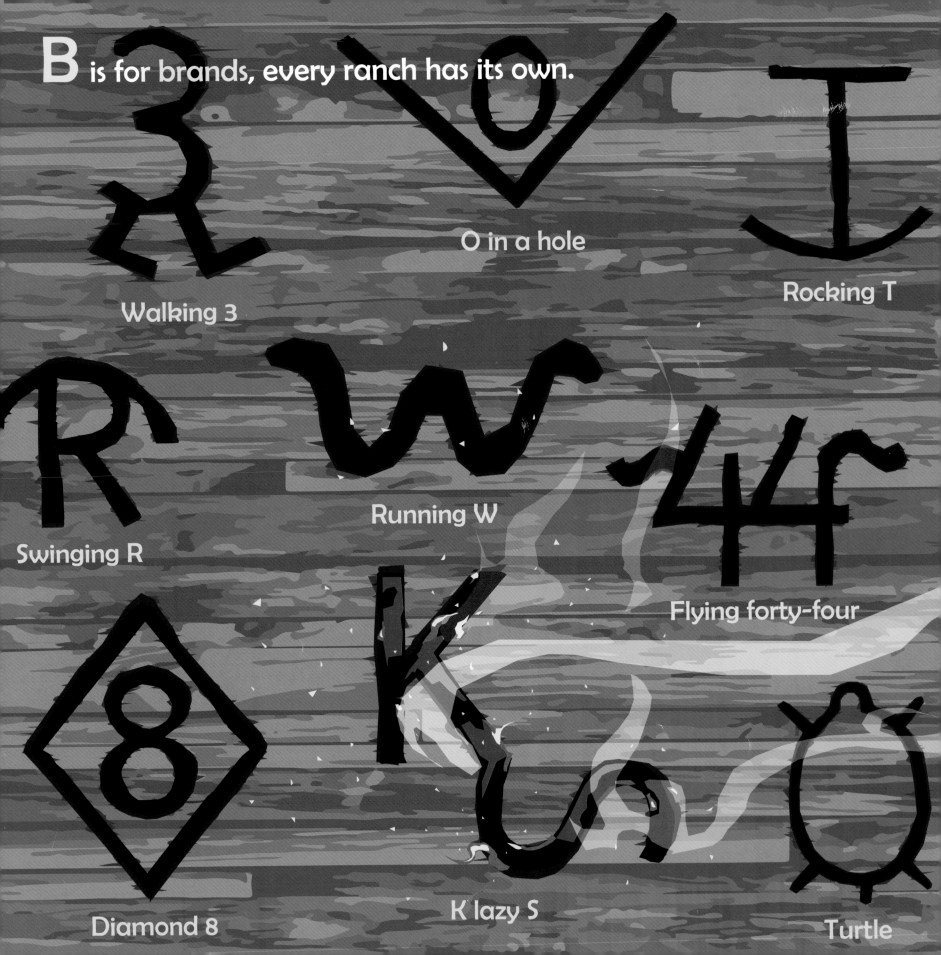

B is for brands, every ranch has its own.

O in a hole

Rocking T

Walking 3

Running W

Swinging R

Flying forty-four

Diamond 8

K lazy S

Turtle

It's a way for the cattle to find their way home.

Seven up

Pig pen

Bow and arrow

Box C

Open hat P

De la Garza

Turkey track

Bar B Q

Crazy A

C is for the cowboys who are skilled bareback riders.

With no saddle or stirrups they must hold on much tighter.

D is for dancing – Country, Western and Rock.
South by Southwest, to Texas they flock.

E is for Enchanted Rock, it wears a pinkish hue.

When you climb up all the way you'll find a gorgeous view.

F is for **Friday night lights**
that shine bright in the fall.

Every week the fans come out
to watch hometown football.

G is for the Gulf Coast, with miles of sandy shore.

Mosey on down and see wildlife galore.

H is for the Hill Country
that gets a burst of blue each spring.

Bluebonnets and wildflowers offer a Texas kind of bling.

I is for **independent**. We fly the Lone Star flag.

You just can't keep a Texan down and for that we like to brag.

J is for the jerseys worn by our favorite teams.

Every year we start fresh with championship dreams.

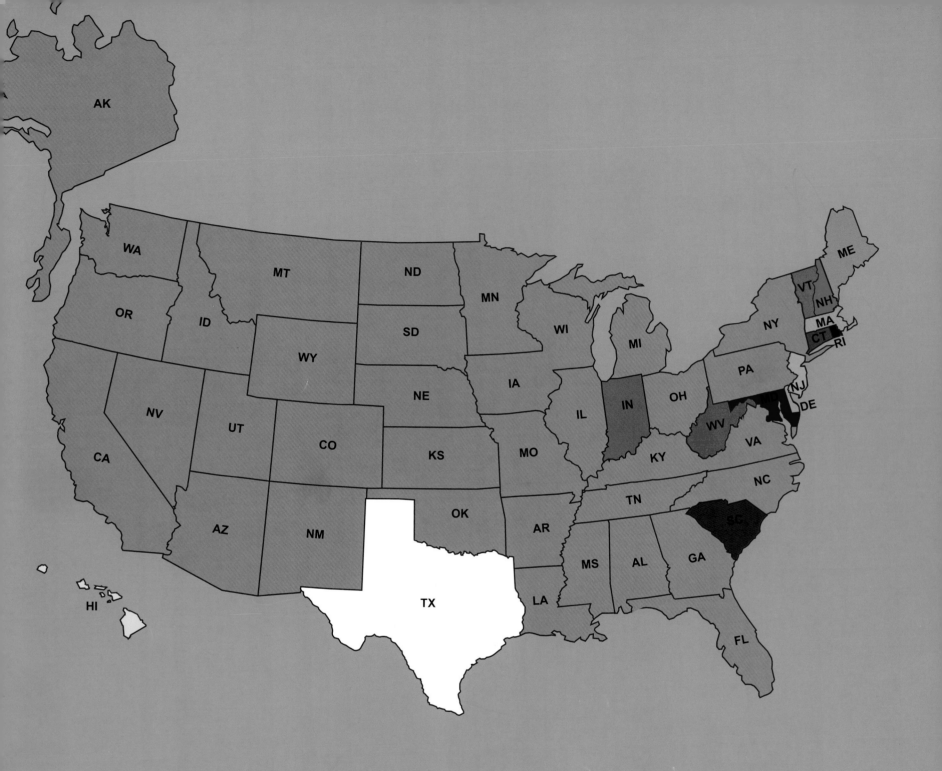

K is for king-sized.

We are bigger, that's correct!

To be as big as our one state, thirteen others must connect.

L is for longhorns with headgear so wide.

Keep 'em doggies moving with a cry of "rawhide!"

M is for the modern art that fills parks and museums.

Spectacular in every way you must come out and see 'em.

O is for oil, "Black Gold" or "Texas Tea."

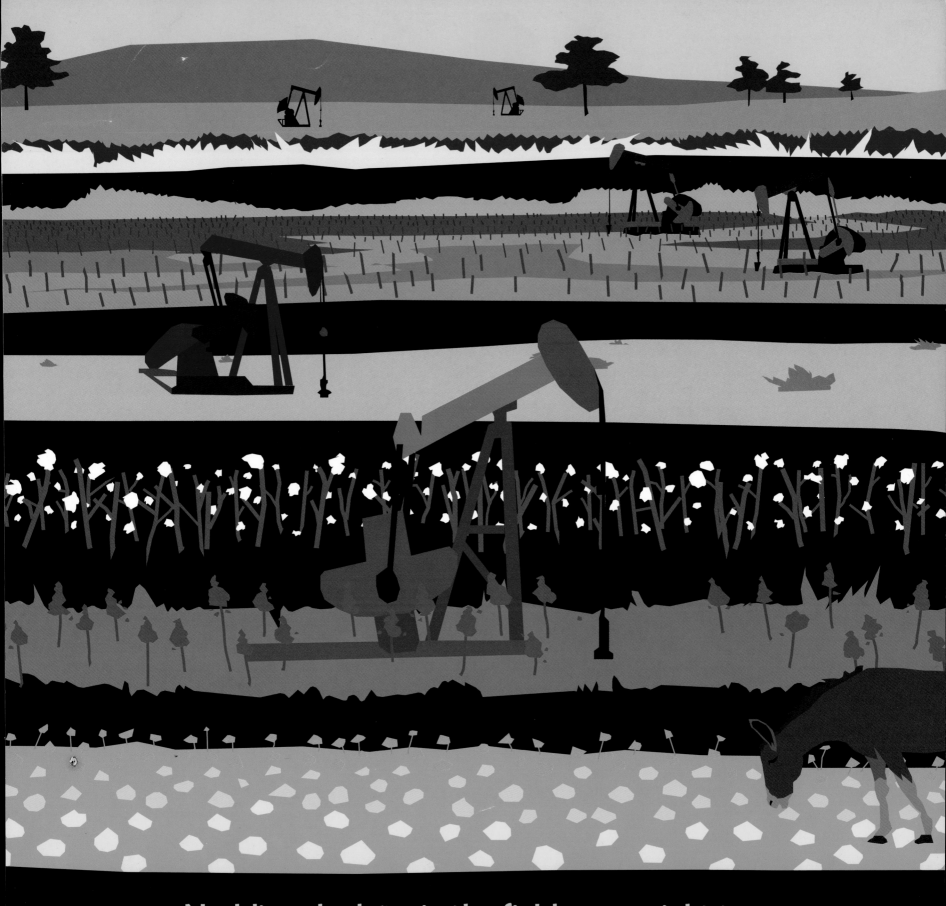

Nodding donkeys in the fields are a sight to see.

P is for the pickup trucks
that drive throughout the town.

They work hard hauling tons of gear,
but are fun with tailgates down.

TEXAS
492

Q is for queso - yummy, gooey, grated cheese.

Sprinkled on a Tex-Mex meal it's guaranteed to please.

R is for the Texas **Rangers** who protected the frontier.

They still wear a white hat and make bad guys disappear.

S is for the State Fair, Big Tex will let you in.

Ride up on the Texas Star
then take the Tower for a spin.

T is for **Texas**, land of wide open spaces.

The big Texas sky covers all kinds of places.

U is for universities, where school spirit is so strong.

Your time there may be short but your memories are lifelong.

V is for Vaqueros,
they sure can rope and ride.

They came up north from Mexico
and now share Texas pride.

W is for windmills,
they pump water
from the ground.

Strong breezes blow across the plains
to make the wheels go' round.

X is for **X**s of the roadrunner's tricky trail.

You can't tell which way he's going unless you see his tail.

FORT WORTH

ROCKWALL

NACOGDOCHES

ROUND ROCK · ODESSA · KELLER · TYLER · DESOTO

CORPUS CHRISTI

FLOWER MOUND

CONROE · PHARR

CEDAR HILL · SAN JUAN

LUBBOCK · GARLAND

GRAPEVINE

HARLINGEN · LEWISVILLE · BEDFORD · COLLEGE STATION · HUNTSVILLE

EDINBURG · AMARILLO · KILLEEN

WACO · LEAGUE CITY

DA

MESQUITE

FARMERS BRANCH

ROSENBERG

PASADENA · GALVESTON

GEORGETOWN · ARLINGTON · PEARLAND · SUGA

TEXARKANA

COPPELL · DENTON · MISSOURI CITY · ABI

SAN ANTOI

BURLESON

COPPERAS COVE

MISSION

CARROLLTON · LONGVIEW · MIDLAND

Y is for *y'all*, as in "Y'all sit down a spell."

HOUSTON

CLEBURNE

LANCASTER

VICTORIA

CEDAR PARK

EL PASO

FRISCO

PORT ARTHUR

LA PORTE

SOCORRO

LUFKIN

WESLACO

AREDO

DUNCANVILLE

SOUTHLAKE

KYLE

NORTH RICHLAND HILLS

MANSFIELD

LLAS

WICHITA FALLS

MCKINNEY

DEER PARK

SHERMAN

SAN MARCOS

LITTLE ELM

FRIENDSWOOD

DEL RIO

THE COLONY

BAYTOWN

BROWNSVILLE

HALTOM CITY

LAND

BEAUMONT

MCALLEN

IRVING

NE

WAXAHACHIE

EULESS

WYLIE

PFLUGERVILLE

TEMPLE

SCHERTZ

IIO

GRAND PRAIRIE

SAN ANGELO

ROWLETT

AUSTIN

PLANO

CLEBURNE

LEANDER

TEXAS CITY

RICHARDSON

NEW BRAUNFELS

HURST

From Houston to Amarillo friendly folks will treat you well.

Z is for the *zig zag* of the river through Big Bend.

Explore the park during the day
and watch stars shine at the end.

Thank you

T is for Thank you, it's not just a letter.
Your help was amazing, it made us much better.

Christopher and Matthew, Meggie, Claire and Libby,
Maureen and Big Daddy.

Thanks to the folks who helped us along the way.
We need the extra eyes, big and little!

The Baumgartners
Stew Fuller
The Grables
Melissa Grobmyer
Maria Howard
The Howingtons
Amy and Peter Malin
The Muzzys
Ann Redding

DonorsChoose.org
Teachers ask. You choose.

A portion of the proceeds from this book
will be donated to literacy programs in
Texas through DonorsChoose.org.